The Original Novella

Guadalupe's Harem

BRIAN C HAILES

Guadalupe's Harem

The Original Novella

Brian C Hailes

Written by Brian C Hailes. Edited by Rick Bennett, Christie Hailes, & Marc R Hunter.

Cover & Interior Artwork by Brian C Hailes.

GUADALUPE'S HAREM: THE ORIGINAL NOVELLA

The infamous Guadalupe has died. Upon his death, his massive inheritence of successful companies, properties, lands, and servants is to fall to his next of living kin, his nephew, Mateo (who never met his deceaced uncle). However, when Mateo leaves his factory life at the behest of Diego, one of Guadalupe's many lawyers, to tour the village compound it becomes apparent that the man who bequeathed Mateo a fortune was indeed a monster. Having employed brutes and traffickers in running his estates and businesses, Guadalupe's former harem of women and children grasp onto Mateo, who becomes embroiled in a dangerous game of inheritence roulette. Can Mateo keep his principles? And even if he does, can he survive the powerful thugs and corrupt businessmen that helped build Guadalupe's nefarious empire?

GUADALUPE'S HAREM

Paperback ISBN: 978-1-951374-18-1
Ebook ISBN: 978-1-951374-61-7

First Edition Published in 2024 by Epic Edge Publishing
www.hailesart.com

Printed in the United States of America

10   9   8   7   6   5   4   3   2   1

Guadalupe's Harem

The Original Novella

Brian C Hailes

$$1$$

"Guadalupe drank himself to death on the night of a solar eclipse," said the messenger. "Or had you already heard?"

Mateo, the warehouse worker, called away early from his graveyard shift and permanently dismissed by his boss to take this meeting, shook his head.

"Some of his servants said it was a sign from the heavens that a new era was about to begin. Others called it justice."

"Justice for what?" asked Mateo.

"You were his nephew, no?"

"Sí." Mateo glanced down at the drink he didn't order from the corner cantina. "But I never met the man."

"Lucky for you." The gentleman with papers, some kind of lawyer, unremarkable in his dress and manner, lifted his own glass and gulped down the last of his hard beverage. "I know what you're thinking. Isn't it a little early in the morning for juicing—?"

"That's not what I was thinking," Mateo said, "I'm only wondering why I was dismissed from the only job I've ever known; why my boss was so upset to see me go, yet so insistent? What did I do wrong?"

"Mateo, Mateo." The lawyer shook his head, sucking through his teeth. "My boy, you did nothing—look, listen, I hesitate to tell you this . . ."

"Please . . . They told me you are a messenger—"

"Diego."

"Sorry, yes, Diego. So, deliver your message."

"Why do you work out here?" Diego asked. "In this oven, this . . . valley of death, that dingy old warehouse? And for so many years? Hard, physical labor making air freighters, shuttles, space transports, or whatever the hell it is you do. For so long you've been at this place, wasting away your days building vessels you'll never travel in. They tell me you've never even been off planet."

"No, you are right. I mean, I would like to." Mateo smiled, then squinted, thinking. "I've worked here for as long as I can remember—I am ashamed to say it, but—even before the legal age. I was abandoned, you see."

"I know you were abandoned, Mateo."

"The work is all I've known. These people at the warehouse, they are my . . . *family*."

"No, my boy," said the lawyer. "No. *Guadalupe* is your family."

"But you told me he's dead."

"Right. Yes."

"Then I do not understand."

Diego took in a long breath and exhaled in frustration. "What do you know about him?" For a gentleman with papers, the lawyer seemed genuinely interested, if not relishing the conversation.

"Not much. From what I've been told, my parents never spoke of him."

Diego nodded. "May their souls find grace."

"What is this about?" asked Mateo. "Did you work for Guadalupe? Did you keep his accounts?"

"On and off. Are you going to drink that?"

Mateo shook his head and slid his full glass across the table. Diego took it and guzzled down the burning draft.

"Guadalupe was a very rich man," said Diego, turning the glass upside-down and slamming it hard over the glazed, wooden finish. "Not your usual testator. And you . . . are his only living relation. Do you follow me, Mateo?"

"Sí."

"No. I don't think you do."

"I told you, I didn't know the man," Mateo said. "Only *of* him. I doubt he even knew I existed."

"But you knew he was your uncle," Diego said again, for confirmation.

"Sí."

Diego sighed, blinked, and raised his overgrown eyebrows. He took out a small ream of neatly prepared papers from his duffle bag, dropping them casually just in front of Mateo.

"My boy, Guadalupe ran a lucrative trade empire, or I should say his people's people ran—er, *run*—said empire. He dealt in a wide variety of industries, handled goods and services both above *and* below the table. Savory, unsavory, he was into a lot of things—*owned* a lot of things. The man's private homestead compound is a village in and of itself. He controlled more assets, more credits, more women, children, servants, workers, beasts than you're even capable of dreaming up."

Mateo's humble gaze met Diego's austere eyes, then moved around them. Only now did he notice the six large men standing as undercover sentry at the outer edges of the small commercial property, their backs all facing inward. "Okay."

"Okay?!"

Mateo shook his head, swallowing. "I assume then, that . . . he has educated people—executives, chairmen, lawyers, such as yourself—sitting around large tables ready to divvy up all those grand assets to the fine folks he's been working with for so long."

"Are you daft, boy?" Diego scoffed. "Guadalupe was not a selfless man. No, he wasn't about to throw his empire to the four stars or allow the government's dogs to seize upon it. No, his instructions were very clear, even iron clad. Only God knows why, but he made sure to keep it all within the family—that thing, that social construct that meant so very *little* to him while there was still air pumping through his lungs."

"He had no family," Mateo said, unable or unwilling to grasp the implications Diego was so vividly making a case for.

"His brother, who is also dead, sired you." Diego's cold stare suggested he very much wanted Mateo to sign Diego's name to what must have been his late uncle's will. He could almost sense the greed for Guadalupe's lucre simmering just below the surface, restrained only by a shallow sense of professional responsibility. "Do you understand what I am telling you, Mateo?"

He swallowed again. "I am beginning to."

"It occurs to me that you are a simple young man who has led a painfully simple life. As an executor of the institution your uncle employed, let me spell it out." Diego took out an old ink pen, and hesitantly handed it across the table to Mateo. "Allow me to make it plain for you. Just about everything Guadalupe had . . . is *yours*."

* * *

Mateo's old life was gone, and he hadn't slept. After taking a few moments to breathe inside the luxury hovercraft that had picked him up from his flat and swept him away, he attempted to put thoughts of home, his friends, and his life at the factory aside to focus on learning about what new obligations he might shoulder, and what drastic life changes lie ahead.

Exiting the limusina, Mateo peered up from the round entry drive to look out over the far side of the compound. "*Exquisite*," he muttered, surprised at the vastness and splendor of the acreage. "I knew it would be grand, but . . ."

Behind him, Diego emerged to escort him on a property tour and introduce him to personnel. Four riders fanned out around the vehicle, parked their hoverbikes at the edge of the grounds, and flanked them as they walked to the reception hall, which was clearly designed, built, and situated to impress all arrivals.

"Are these my bodyguards?" Mateo asked, too much distracted by the men's proximity to fully appreciate the view.

"Guadalupe never went anywhere without them," said Diego.

"Hm, not even the baño?"

Not so much as a courtesy laugh.

"This way," Diego said, "I will introduce you to 'The Wall,' *Bruno*, our head of house security, and we will take breakfast."

As they entered through the center of a three-arch stone portal into a great circular gallery, a man in a dark suit walked straight toward them, holding out his gloved, four-fingered hand.

"Bruno Salazar," the man said, his heavy grip dwarfing Mateo's. A diagonal scar spanned the man's face from forehead to chin, and tattoos of dozens of big cats coated his thick neck.

"Mateo. Pleasure."

"Bruno keeps the peace," Diego said, "takes out the garbage, watches the perimeter, and oversees the training program for new recruits."

"New recruits?" Mateo asked.

Bruno pointed to a large outdoor patio where several perfectly formed lines of fighters practiced hand-to-hand combat on the grass. "We take private security very seriously; it was upmost on Guadalupe's list of priorities."

"With a property like this," Mateo said, "I can see why."

Bruno smiled and corrected him. "*Many* properties."

"Right."

Bruno pulled out a box of fine cigars and offered one to Mateo.

"Thank you," Mateo said, "But no."

"These are the finest cigars money can buy. One does not say "no" to Guadalupe's finest."

Mateo breathed deeply. "And yet I must."

At that, Bruno and Diego exchanged unhappy glances. "Do not be deceived by the calm, hermano," Bruno said. "There is an unspoken war here."

"War?"

"Sí. Guadalupe made a lot of money, secured many assets, and kept a harem of lovely ladies—wherever he went. He also made many enemies. To be frank, I was surprised to learn Guadalupe's demise came by his own hand. I did warn him he drank too much."

"Hm," Mateo didn't know what to say.

"Of course, I mean no disrespect," said Bruno, as they exited the entry hall, descended a curving marble staircase, and moved on over a wide path cutting through a field of healthy, freshly cut and watered grass.

"It's fine," said Mateo. "As I told Diego, I barely knew of the man."

"I knew him plenty," said Bruno. "You're probably wondering how I acquired this great scar."

Mateo said nothing, so Bruno continued. "Guadalupe gave it to me in one of the rare moments he was actually sober. He used my own hunting knife."

Still, Mateo kept his mouth shut.

"Why, may you ask? I insulted his intelligence."

"So, he had a temper," Mateo said.

"That would be a gross understatement," said Diego. "However, without it, he would not have acquired all this. The man truly made negotiation into an art form. He could intimidate any industrial titan with a mere glance. And any man, woman, or child would do his bidding by the point of his finger, even fall on their own sword . . . or someone else's."

Mateo stopped a moment, forcing the others to as well. *These guys really think I'm a simpleton.* "I appreciate the added insight; sounds like my uncle was a *lovely* man."

Bruno grinned. "Some of the servants swear he *wasn't* a man."

"Let us eat," said Diego. "The cocineros have been busy all morning."

As they entered the cook house, Mateo thought he had wandered into one of the fine luxury restaurants or pastry shops he had only seen in pictures. Rows and rows of culinary masterpieces lined glass-covered shelves as if on display for art lovers or star-gazing wine-tasting tours.

"Everything is made fresh daily," Diego said, "Per Guadalupe's strict requirements."

Mateo stared at a few of the pastries before making eye contact with what might have been the primary chef. The portly man smiled back. "In my experience," said the cocinero, "When it comes to donuts and cookies, the best way to remove them from temptation's way . . . is to *eat* them."

"A sentiment no doubt shared by Guadalupe himself," Diego said with a forced chuckle as he paraded Mateo past a few of the other chefs, their heaping trays of pastries and steaming appetizers, and on through the open kitchen and outdoor dining patio.

Another cocinero stepped forward and managed to shove some type of warm sugary croissant into his grasp. Mateo studied the cinnamon-sprinkled morsel, sniffed it, and took a small bite, savoring its doughy sweetness as he gazed out upon the emerging landscape that—so far as Diego had him believing—now belonged to him. *"Wow."*

"Yes, it is something." Diego obviously referred to the impressive buildings and grounds and not the savory pastry, all of which proved worthy of praise. Diego and Bruno also took some food in passing, but Bruno peeled off to return to the business of his trainees.

As Mateo and the lawyer strode along a central white stone path, the sea sparkled to the east, begging to be sailed. A cool breeze cut through the heat, causing the myriad palms, well-manicured bushes, and other vegetation and flora to sway as if in a dance across the perfectly kept yard. Spires and domes of swirling rock, handsome lodgings, cottages, footbridges, and waterfalls intermingled with terraces of grapes and olives stretched far. Mateo wondered what more could be added to such an exotic paradise that had been Guadalupe's village compound. Now it belonged to Mateo. But how could this be?

A man even burlier than Bruno approached them and introduced himself. "You must be Mateo. I am Javier. I am the cleaner, and I will make your house new." They shook hands, and he bowed, but kept his eyes locked on Mateo, as if sizing him up—or down.

"Nice to meet you," said Mateo.

"The pleasure is mine. You know, you look like him. Well, a younger, healthier version."

"Your title, what does it mean?" Mateo asked. *"Cleaner?"*

Javier glanced at Diego, suppressing a reaction before answering. "I uh, supervise the hacienda, and everything that goes on. Large estates like this one require order. And sometimes there are messes that need to be—"

"Cleaned up," Mateo said.

"Consequently—"

"The *cleaner*." Mateo nodded, but inside he balked at the uneasy feeling in his gut as he worked through what possible 'messes' Javier could be referring to. The man, after all, gave off the impression of a mobster's muscle or a gangster's lap dog. If there was a corpse that needed to be disposed of, it wasn't a far stretch to imagine this man standing at Guadalupe's back door. Diego also mentioned something about Bruno 'taking out the garbage,' and Mateo wondered where Javier's 'cleaning' ended and Bruno's 'waste disposal' duties began.

"Then I shall call on you," Mateo said jokingly, "If anyone ever spills the Sangria."

The three men chuckled, and Diego and Mateo continued down the stone path to tour the property's far reaches. "Of course, we usually use shuttles, hoverboards, or bikes to get about," Diego said, "but I thought you might like to see everything on foot for your initial visit."

"Yes, it's fine. Taking it all in. Thank you."

"I would also like for you to meet the overseer of the plantation," Diego said. "His name is Hugo. He lives under the central tower, and he has the energy of a fire rat."

"Fire rat?"

"You'll see. He also keeps watch over the harem."

Like Bruno and Javier, Hugo boasted a significant physical presence, but with a personality to dwarf the others. Cheeks as shiny red as emergency blinkers on commuter trains, he met Mateo with a mighty hug. "We're so glad to have you!" His voice boomed, and he nearly lifted Mateo off the ground, causing him to wonder if he had treated Guadalupe this way. Mateo could almost feel Diego shaking his head in disgust behind them.

"Come, before you get settled in," Hugo said, "let me introduce you to Guadalupe's spicy selection of servants and concubines."

"*Spicy?*"

"Sí. *Picante.* Only the best for the one with the most. They are beautiful, seductive, trained in all the appetites of the body and beyond."

"Beyond?" Mateo asked.

"My boy, there is the physical . . . and the *metaphysical.*" The huge man chuckled a raspy, guttural roar. "They will play with your mind, your insecurities, and your sensibilities like the angel harpers pluck their strings, ever leaving you wanting more."

Mateo could only raise his eyebrows at such a pitch.

Hugo and the gentleman with papers led Mateo down a curving flight of stone steps toward the beach, where off to one side stood a series of at least two dozen stone dwellings built together and stacked in an alternating pattern against the sprawling cliffs overlooking the waters below.

The low rumble and distant echo of an air freighter—one that Mateo had likely helped build—shot off into the atmosphere across the late-afternoon sky, and Mateo pondered how his life could have changed so drastically and so unexpectedly.

"Per Guadalupe's written instructions," Diego said, "Hugo and I will introduce you to the full menu this first night, and you will stay in the master's chambers, even Guadalupe's 'royal suite'."

"'*Royal* suite?'" Mateo said. "Was he—?"

Diego scoffed. "That's what he called it."

A bit pretentious, Mateo thought, to deem oneself *royalty,* no matter one's assets or accomplishments. *But then, I suppose we are all children and potential heirs of the Creator.*

"You will think yourself a royal as well when my courtesans are through with you," Hugo piped.

They really don't know who they're dealing with, Mateo thought.

As they approached the beach, Mateo counted 35 servants standing in a row parallel to the white sand shoreline. They all looked down, hands at their sides, humble servants that carried the air of slaves. Yet they were all clean, well—if sparsely—clothed, and styled to compete with even the most elegant of model and fashion icons from the periodicals Mateo had read on his limited breaks at the warehouse.

These people, mostly young women, along with several children, were beautiful—something even Hugo's flowery words had not prepared him for—yet a profound melancholy permeated their collective demeanor. And something deeply disturbing cut at him.

One black-haired, dark-complexioned girl stood out, and he caught himself staring. Her face downcast, she said nothing.

"*These* are my…?" Mateo didn't want to say 'workers,' 'servants,' 'slaves,' or 'escorts' out loud in their presence.

So, Hugo did it for him: "*Night servants*—the world's best. Aren't they *pretty?*"

"*Night servants.*" Mateo echoed the words quietly, not knowing how else to respond.

"Sí." Diego stopped and faced the line, his hands and digital pad at his back. "They are all yours. Bought and paid for. Once beholden to Guadalupe's every whim, now to *yours.*"

Slaves indeed, Mateo thought. *But not for long.*

Two other men with beautifully dark complexions and brilliant white dress, each with the figure of a bodybuilder, stepped forward to escort Mateo and the lawyer before Guadalupe's lineup.

Guards, Mateo figured, eyeing the jungle hunter machetes sheathed at their waists. The black-coated, stainless-steel blades with sawback spines looked cruel, even primitive considering the plasma and weapons technologies employed on even the most basic handheld weapons stored in the safes on most of the space transport vessels Mateo had built. These blades were not meant to stun or vaporize; they were meant to scar, maim, and intimidate.

"Take your pick," said the executor. "Guadalupe's instructions were very clear, and you signed the papers."

Mateo glanced at each one of them in turn, from the far left, to just in front of him, and on to the far right, his gaze again lingering on the dark-haired girl.

Hugo must have noticed his tarrying eyes and said, "That one's Ana—one of Guadalupe's favorites. Quite the looker, eh?"

Mateo shot him a sidelong glare. "I wish for them to be freed."

Diego exhaled sharply. "I do not think you understand what you have here, Mateo. This is who and what they are. You cannot merely dismiss—"

"I can," said Mateo. "And I must. Please, send them back to their beds, and in the morning, we can sort this out."

"I'm afraid I cannot," said Diego. "The will and testament, my superiors, the order and workings of this compound. There is a system Guadalupe put in place, expectations—"

"Yes," Hugo added. "Certain way things are done."

"Undo them," Mateo said, fully realizing how naïve he must have sounded.

"But Mateo," the lawyer replied. "I do not think you grasp the gravity of the situation, the responsibility on your shoulders. It will take time. Please."

"All they have known is servitude," said Hugo. "All they have known is *Guadalupe*. You are his blood. He wanted you to fill his boots, take his mantle. And he wanted you *here*. With them." The man gestured with his fat hands toward the young women and children, as though he were advertising the latest land speeder or luxury yacht.

"Are the servants paid?" Mateo asked, nearly cringing at the thought of these innocents at the behest of any man, let alone someone as rich, powerful (and infamous, if the break-time stories were true) as his uncle.

"What does that matter?" Hugo asked, confused.

Mateo's cold stare pressed him.

"Uh, yes," Diego interjected. "They earn a-a modest living allowance, room, board. Necessities."

Mateo patted Diego on the shoulder. "Then we shall find them a more respectable employment. Tomorrow. Yes, tomorrow, we'll inquire as to their talents and interests."

"I hesitate to tell you this," Diego said, "but I'm afraid we will be much too busy to focus on such trivial matters. No, we'll be taking the private transport off planet. Let me give special assignment to our employment specialists, as well as Hugo here—”

“Thank you for the suggestion,” Mateo said. “But I insist.”

Clutching his digital pad against his chest as though fighting the urge to look up suggested response protocols under unusual circumstances, Diego glanced back at the guards before facing Mateo again. “Fine. Sure.”

Mateo made to leave, but Diego stopped him with a firm hand on his shoulder. “My boy, please, Guadalupe’s instructions first—”

“Oh, yes,” Mateo said. “The papers. I’m to select . . .?”

“As many as you want,” Hugo chimed. “Whomever you want. Perhaps that lovely young blossom there?”

Mateo sighed and looked out across the gathering. He pointed to three of the young women who seemed to be the oldest in the group and closest to his own age, the brunette girl that had caught his eye—*Ana*—among them.

“Very good choices, Mateo,” Hugo said. “Are you sure you don’t want another? Perhaps one of the young ones?”

Mateo shook his head.

“Yes,” Diego chimed in, as though he were taking mental note of his selections. “*Ana, Maria,* and *Lucia.*”

Even the lawyer knew their names. The unsettling nature of this entire exchange made Mateo want to fill the men’s pockets with the servants’ tears and be rid of them. Yet this lineup wasn’t Diego’s, but Guadalupe’s.

“I’m tired,” said Mateo, and he slowly walked back toward the stone staircase. The three young women followed, tailed by the guards, Hugo, the lawyer, and the unchosen ones, who, like trained pets, quietly broke off and returned to their individual lodgings. Simple, humble, stacked lodgings.

* * *

The ‘royal suite’ proved even more ostentatious than Mateo anticipated, yet he couldn’t help but appreciate the magnificent space, its eloquent architecture, and attention to detail. Only Mateo and the three selected young women had entered its doors, but somehow, he knew the guards and overseers weren’t afar off.

Mateo was instantly struck by a dizzying chorus of sweet scents. All around them were handsome stonework, glass cases, chandeliers, polished marble floors and pillars. With towering ceilings, it looked like an exotic desert palace, its open-air waterfalls, showers, and pools indeed suited for kings.

An enormous open bar teeming with liquors, tequilas, wines, alien brews, and drafts, all exhibited in expensive bottles or from decorative taps drew everyone's attention.

"Care for a drink?" Maria asked, sauntering over. "You must be thirsty. We have some exotic juices. Something fruity? Cold?"

"No but thank you." He was thirsty, but if he drank anything, he thought he might have to prepare it himself to be safe.

She lifted a bottle of fine wine. "Are you sure? *Nothing?*"

"Not for me, no." Mateo peered up at the high archways and stirring ceiling frescoes resembling cloudy skies in baby blue and every other color of the rainbow in subtle accent. As they slowly made their way into the main area and bedchamber, the girls approached Mateo and began to undress him. He lifted his hands and backed away from them. "Whoa, what are you doing?"

"You need to be cleaned," said Ana matter-of-factly.

"Do you prefer a shower?" Maria asked. "Or a bath?"

Mateo looked around, noticing only one very large bed up a few steps on the far side of the great room, and no other sleeping arrangements save a loveseat and couch in the space out by the bar. A plethora of gigantic throw pillows and whisps of flower petals also dotted the candle-lit area as though the place had been prepared a honeymoon suite.

Lucia stepped forward, dropping her gown. "Do we not please you?"

Mateo strode forward and knelt, lifting, and replacing the gown back over her slender shoulders. "You are all stunning, and I would be so lucky, but I come from a very different world; one where I believe there are consequences to our actions. Why don't we first get to know one another in the traditional sense?"

"The *traditional* sense?" asked Maria.

Mateo's face lighted. "By talking."

"But you still need to be cleaned," said Ana. "Shall we clean you while you talk?"

"Do I smell?" he asked with a grin, to which she did not answer. "I suppose I have been walking around all day. But thank you. I can manage on my own."

"Is it really true?" Lucia asked, "that everything Guadalupe owned is now . . . *yours?*"

"Is that what they're saying in the servant's quarters?" Mateo asked.

"Is it not true?" Ana suddenly looked concerned.

"Doesn't feel like anything's changed," said Mateo. "I'm just out of my element, and I believe I've taken on . . . a great risk. However, I'm more complicated than they think."

"What do you mean?"

Mateo thought a moment before shaking his head. "Forget it."

"What is your preference?" Maria asked.

"My preference for what?" Mateo blinked. "To what do you refer?"

"What would you like us to do? We can dance. Play. Sing. If you want to participate . . . or simply watch—?"

Ana glanced over at the other girls, and they seemed to communicate without words.

Mateo looked up at the immaculate bed. "Why don't you all sleep there, or on these pillows here. I'll, uh, I'll take the couch by the bar . . ." Again, she caught his eye. "After I go clean myself up, I suppose," he added.

Plunging waterfalls cascaded from the roof of the artificial cavern where Mateo lounged in the middle of three stacked bathing pools. He moved his sore feet through the brimming blue water and rubbed off the sweat of the day, unbelieving of his plight. Just as he rose naked from the water, in walked one of the girls.

"*Lucia,*" he gasped, dropping back below the surface. "What are you doing?"

She stared at him with purpose. "Taking this off." Again, she slipped the gown from over her shoulders and stepped forward.

"I told you . . ." he said, looking away, "There's no need."

"*But there is.*" She approached him resolutely.

"Can I ask you a question first?"

She shrugged her consent, stepping ever so gracefully. "You can ask me anything."

Mateo hesitated. "Have you been ordered—*coerced* to seduce me? What did Hugo tell you all before I arrived?"

Lucia swallowed as she slowly and elegantly entered the pool and drew closer. "It would be safer for all of us if you—"

"Give in?" Mateo guessed.

Lucia truly looked at him for the first time. "Yes."

"When you say *safer*," Mateo backed away slowly, "It makes me think you've been lied to. I see only an illusion . . . a *cage*.

Her downcast gaze confirmed Mateo's suspicions.

Maria, too, entered the room, carrying a drink and wearing mauve-colored lingerie designed and worn with unmistakable purpose. And then Ana appeared in a brilliant white number that complemented Maria's well.

Mercy, Mateo thought. *Perhaps a bath wasn't the best idea under the circumstances.*

The three converged on him as sirens to a shipwrecked sailor stranded on the shoals, their fingernails, and glistening bodies like tickling tentacles all around him. It took all he had to keep from staring at their perky breasts.

Summoning every ounce of will, he gently pushed them off. "Please, ladies, I only want to talk. I know why you are doing this, and I'm here to tell you—you don't have to."

"Do you not find us . . . *desirable?*" Ana pressed up against him, her breath intoxicating.

Mateo sighed deeply, again pressing out of their grasp, and he exited the pool.

"What have we done wrong?" asked Maria, moving to the edge and balancing the drink.

"Nothing." Mateo started dressing. "I mean, I know what this place is; I know what Guadalupe built here, and I'm aware of his . . . *expectations* . . . for all of us. It's just that I'm not him. Please do not make the mistake of treating me like you treated your old jefe."

And he left to make his bed on the couch . . . *alone.*

* * *

The moonlight rays shone through open portals, and a gentle breeze snuck in. The calming, soothing pressure on Mateo's back—like someone's massaging touch—put him to sleep and woke him simultaneously. He stirred, rolled over, and glanced up to the silhouette of a young woman, *Ana*, peering down at him from the couch.

Had he fallen on the floor during the night?

Startled, he sat up and fumbled backward against a pillar. Looking around, he caught his breath. "What's the matter? What's happening?" He stood, and she mirrored his movements, drawing close.

"Why aren't you sleeping?" he asked.

"Can't sleep." Her stunning eyes wandered from her feet to the tiled floor and across the barren walls until finally resting at Mateo's chest.

"It's the middle of the night."

"I know . . . Do you want me, Mateo?"

"Yes," he said softly. "But not like this. Look at me."

At length, she did, but only for a moment; some inner turmoil prevented her from meeting his eyeline. It didn't seem to stop her before when she was with the other girls in the bath.

"Do I *look* like Guadalupe?"

Her gaze, again, wandered. "Only a little."

"Never mind," Mateo let out a sigh. "Whatever you were used to having to do with—or *for*—that man . . . well, that's all in the past. Okay?"

Mateo reached down to gently take her by the hand, but when they touched, she flinched and trembled, so he let go. "Sorry. I'm—I'm sorry," he said. "It's all right. I won't hurt you."

She gasped as though fearing she had offended him and offered her trembling hand. When he didn't take it, she untied the front of her frock, revealing the center strip of her bare torso underneath.

"No, no," Mateo said. "Please. That's not necessary; you don't owe me anything."

Motioning for her to stop undressing, their eyes finally met, an understanding reached.

She slowly began to re-tie her gown, and Mateo held out a guiding arm behind her back to escort her back to the master's suite with Maria and Lucia. "You don't owe yourself to anyone. Not anymore. You are free."

She gave a slight nod. However, Mateo wondered if she truly believed him. Perhaps in time she could regain a man's trust, and even learn what real love meant.

Mateo wasn't even sure he understood it.

Yet one thing had become abundantly clear: For a man famed far and wide for his great wealth and influence, Guadalupe left behind fruits exhibiting a lack in character as only the most debased or morally destitute Mateo had met or heard of. And a slew of henchmen to carry on his tarnishing work. A tiny sliver of fear stuck inside and began to split Mateo's mind. Whether his well-being would come into question—or already had—he knew he had a mission to perform, and it would not be without its dangers.

He put Ana to bed with the others and watched over them until they were all asleep, then returned to his own pillow by the couch.

* * *

Late into the morning, after the suns had ascended, Mateo escorted Ana, Maria, and Lucia to the cook house and told them to order anything they like from the cocineros.

Diego joined them along the way, digital pad in hand. "This is most unusual, Mateo. Guadalupe never took such company for breakfast."

"Get used to unusual," Mateo answered. "Speaking of which, will you please have Hugo summon the others from the beach last night, including the guards? I'd like for them to also enjoy a hearty meal with us. And I would also like to speak with my new accountant and CFO as soon as possible. Can you get me their numbers?"

"To what end?" asked Diego, obviously struggling to understand Mateo's motives. The lawyer pulled him aside curtly. "Mateo, what is it you are trying to accomplish here? Are you trying to cause a stir? Upset the established order of things? I warn you, stepping on the overseers' toes would not be an advisable course."

"Is that a threat?" Mateo asked.

"Only counsel. I assure you; your energies will be better spent sticking to our outlined schedule. We are to visit the company headquarters, meet the conglomerates, and make an appearance to a selection of Guadalupe's prized side-businesses, their executives, and employees. They are expecting us, you see. Finally, you will get your chance to travel beyond this stale atmosphere."

"I will make a visit to company headquarters," Mateo said, "and meet the executives. In good time—not today. I would like to set things straight here at home before looking outward. You know, get a handle on the place."

Either turning red from his growing anger or the splash of sunrise colors on Diego's skin, he couldn't be sure, but Mateo would have to be on high alert from this point on.

"I will get you their numbers," Diego relented, "so long as you tell me what you plan to do."

"Fantastic. Will you join us?"

He seethed, uttering sarcastically, "Do I have a choice?"

Mateo straightened with a nod. "Sí. You have your agency."

Hugo ushered in the servants, who all looked bewildered as they sat next to the three girls in the fine dining area of the cookhouse, and the burly, red-cheeked man took a silent meeting with Diego out on the patio. Mateo watched them closely as they left, conversed, and ultimately returned, both unsatisfied.

"Is there something I need to know?" Mateo asked Diego.

"No, no," he said with a manufactured smile, "We were just going over the changes to itinerary."

"Right," Mateo said, seeing through his lie. "Of course."

He turned to the servants. "Order what you like—as much as you like. It seems you could all use a good meal."

Then back to Diego. "Please send for Bruno, his fighting men, and Javier . . . also, any other 'cleaners' I was not blessed to meet yesterday."

"But they are on their own schedules," Diego contested. "Many of them work through the night, you see—and, might I say, it is not wise to allow so many to mingle at once."

"Not wise?" Mateo repeated. "No, you may not say, Diego . . . *Be careful.*"

To that, he clearly took offense. "*Careful—?*"

Hugo, watching the uncomfortable exchange, broke in to change the subject. "Tell us, Mateo, uh, how was your night?"

Mateo exhaled sharply and faced the nosy man. "How my night went is none of your business, Hugo."

He too took offense as many of the servants tried to conceal their grins, but he concealed it better than Diego—with a hearty laugh. "Yes, yes, I understand, Mateo—but with three such beauties—Lucia, there, she will light any man's candle until he becomes a wildfire, yes? For tomorrow, perhaps you can try Sofia and Isabella. They are sisters, twins; two for the price of one, eh?"

Mateo stood from his bench with a scowl. "Nothing happened last night if you must know! We slept! In separate rooms! And this talk is inappropriate. They are sitting *right there!* Have you no grasp of humanity? Civility? There will be no more talk of these people as property. Everyone here will respect *everyone here,* or you or I die today. Do you understand what I am telling you hombre?

Dropping his gaze, Hugo gritted his teeth, and uttered quietly, "Yes, Mateo. My apologies. I meant no disrespect."

Mateo looked around at everyone gathered, a heavy, tangible tension hovering in the air, and varying levels of fear on their faces. Perhaps there was more of Guadalupe in him than he thought.

Even the cocineros had paused their busy preparations to gawk at the exchange.

Hugo stared angrily at the girls, as though letting them know retribution for their actions—or lack thereof—would come later.

"Don't look at them, hermano," Mateo said. "Look at me. They are not at fault here."

He nodded, relenting to Mateo's official supremacy, if not the physical. Yet a hint of rebellion lingered there.

At length, everyone's downcast eyes slowly rose to settle on Mateo.

He drew in a long breath and let it out slowly. It seemed everyone wanted to know what he was going to say next. Everyone but Ana. She just stared up at him with admiration.

"Let's eat," he said, before quietly sitting down.

* * *

Even the baños here are exquisite, Mateo thought, trying to get his mind off his blow-up at Hugo in front of everyone over breakfast. Never had he allowed his temper to get the better of him to such a degree, not at home, not with his friends, not even at the warehouse.

Eventually, the servants, Javier and his people, and Bruno with his fighting men—once they all had food in their bellies—got on to a thousand wonders, and the breakfast party became a jovial affair, despite the brooding expressions of Hugo, Diego, and several of the others holding positions of power under Guadalupe's regime.

It was clear to Mateo there would have to be changes made in management, but to make them too quickly would be a mistake. There was much more by way of observation to do before making any big moves—a process that would likely take weeks if not months to accomplish the needed vicissitudes properly, strategically.

Those certain individuals, Mateo would have to watch. And *closely.*

"Alvaro is a cautious one," Diego had told him when Mateo asked after the surly fellow sitting across from him and the girls. And— "If you need a warrior, Andrés is your man."

How Mateo would remember everyone's names and faces, he had no idea. How does one adopt an entire homestead, village, and trade empire overnight?

Of all the magnificent spaces within Guadalupe's impressive compound, the baño turned out to be Mateo's favorite. Only because he was alone, not being watched or tested, and not having to memorize any pertinent social or business-related information. As Mateo sat on the toilet, he heard the ever-so-subtle opening and closing of a door—and not the same door he had entered through. No footfalls thereafter. Or creaking cubicle hinges. *Odd.*

Was there someone inside the baño with him? Or was he still alone?

Lowering his head, he listened more closely.

A faint echo of the festivities outside.

A drip from one of the sinks.

A breath.

Not his.

A dark figure burst through the door of his stall and seized upon him!

Guarding with his arms, Mateo's strength was no match for his attacker's, and a vice-like grip instantly closed over his neck. Fighting and kicking, Mateo flailed about desperately. Lifted off the seat, and thrown out of the stall, Mateo's back slammed against a sink and the wall behind it. He curled onto the floor in pain but glanced up just in time to get belted across the face.

"You are nothing like Guadalupe," the man raged.

Mateo spat blood and coughed, and a relentless leg kicked him hard in the ribs again and again. He curled into a ball trying to protect himself from the onslaught as he heard a ruckus of others entering the fray. When the physical assaults on Mateo finally abated, he cautiously peered up to look.

Three men, one of them, Javier, had seized upon Hugo, and held him fast, dragging him backward toward the door. "Let go," Hugo huffed. "Let me go. Let me go! I'll kill 'im. I'll—"

With much effort, they wrestled the enormous brute outside, kicking and thrashing, the door slamming shut behind them, and Mateo was again left alone, blood dripping from his mouth onto his hands and the fine tile floor. Exhaling, he closed his eyes and gently touched at his throbbing head and side. Then he crumpled over.

*　*　*

"Won't you be pressing charges?" Javier asked Mateo.

"No."

After having gathered himself up off the bloody restroom floor, and staggering outside following the incident, the onsite doctor whisked him off to the infirmary to attend to his wounds. Despite the insistence he rest, Mateo instead called for a hoverchair to allow him to continue his tour of the vast property—if only to try and move past the bad business with Hugo. He would meet more of the staff and find the extent to which the boundaries of his new territory ended. He also wanted to send a message that it would take more than a fistfight and a few kicks to the ribs to bring down their new head of household. Of course, he had succinctly fired and banned Hugo from the compound as he couldn't have anyone under his employ he couldn't trust, let alone someone willing to attack, physically harm him, and dish out death threats.

Unhappy as he was to be veering off-schedule Diego had obliged him on a second day of unscheduled rounds and cancelled or pushed back his other appointments and business meetings off planet.

Mateo had also asked Ana and the other two girls to accompany them on their extended property tour, and they seemed content enough to come along.

"I would like to visit the plantation first," said Mateo. "Is that not where Hugo resided?"

"It is," Diego answered. "Through the beekeeper's shed? Or by way of the cliffs?"

"I've already seen the cliffs," said Mateo.

"Past Genna's then," said Javier.

"Genna?" Mateo asked.

"Don't pay her any heed, amigo," said Javier. "She's loco. Nobody speaks to her . . . unless they need honey. She's the beekeeper."

"I see. You know, Javier, I've been meaning to thank you."

"No thanks necessary, hermano," he said.

"Hugo could have killed me back there."

"Sí."

"Why did you and your men intervene?"

Javier smiled. "I'm the cleaner . . . And he was spilling blood on my floor."

Mateo nodded. Upon their meeting, he had simply grouped him in with the thuggish Bruno and Hugo. "I misjudged you, Javier."

"It happens," he said.

As they approached the apiary, Diego and Javier led out, following a stony path over a footbridge, garden, and field of hives.

"Welcome to the bee yard," said Javier, glancing back. "Genna! You have visitors!"

A tiny woman emerged from a cottage nearly devoured by wild vegetation, bees swarming around her by the hundreds.

Mateo eyed the several swarms across the many beehives and garden flowers. "Are these bees—?"

"Dangerous?" Diego said. "No. They're genetically modified."

Maria leaned close to Mateo. "No stingers," she whispered.

"I wager they told you I'm crazy," said Genna, as she approached. "It's true. My mind is a council of radishes. And if someone offends me, I claw their eyes out. You must be the new honcho."

"Claw their eyes out?" Mateo cocked his head slightly to one side. "Not really."

She grinned, "No, not really." However, something in her mischievous look betrayed that answer and left Mateo on edge.

"We're showing him the plantation," said Diego. "Just passing by."

"What is that?" Mateo asked, pointing across the field at a large stone building barely visible through a thick mess of trees, vines, and shrubbery at a distance.

The other girls dropped their gaze. Genna's jaw tensed from the effort of keeping silent. Mateo could tell she was holding something back.

"It's nothing," said Diego. "An old storage shed. Derelict. Abandoned."

That sounded like a deflection to Mateo, who noticed the split in the trail up ahead, the path leading to the building much less travelled, and overgrown with grass. "I want to see it." He turned and moved toward the mysterious structure.

"But the plantation is *this* way," said Javier from behind. "Mateo? . . . Ay, ay, ay."

Everyone eventually followed.

Despite the warmth of the day, the bright and clear sky, something of cold dread emanated from the shadowy stone walls lurking behind the vegetation as they approached.

Ducking under hanging branches, Mateo followed the path around and to what must have been the front of the small warehouse-sized building.

Mateo reached for the handle of a rusty metal door with a keypad. "Locked? . . . *Please*." He motioned for Diego to open it.

"Mateo, I must insist we continue our tour—"

"This *is* the tour," Mateo said, growing tired of Diego's attitude.

Diego swallowed, nodded, and stepped forward to enter a five-digit code which caused the large swinging door to open on its squeaky hinges.

Mateo gulped and moved his hoverchair forward into the dark space lit only by a series of small round windows lining the high interior walls. Spotlight rays shone through at parallel angles, lighting rows of wooden beds positioned along each wall, as though the space had been set up as a vintage-style infirmary. However, something told Mateo, this was, and had never been, a hospital.

He gulped again as he entered the main area, the eerie silence making the soft footfalls behind him unsettling.

"Do I even have to ask?" Mateo said.

Diego cleared his throat. "These were the old servants' quarters. As you can see, they've since been moved and upgraded."

"You said it was a storage shed."

"Yes. That is what it's been used for in the interim."

Mateo looked around. "Besides the beds, there's nothing being stored here. It's completely empty."

Diego shook his head, he too, looking around, as if for the first time. "You would have to ask Hugo. This was under his purview."

"Strange for a servant's lodging to be missing a kitchen, laundry . . . a baño. Don't you think?" He aimed the comment at Diego, who seemed to ignore him, until he answered. "As I'm told, food was delivered them, and they did their business outside."

"Genna?" Mateo asked.

She shook her head like a good servant. "I never come here . . . anymore."

"Girls?" He looked over at Ana, Maria, and Lucia.

"Yes?" Lucia asked, stepping forward.

"Did you stay here?"

All three girls shook their heads in the negative, avoiding eye contact, yet their ticks and reactions to one another sent mixed signals. Either they were lying, or Mateo didn't believe them. The overseers' hold over them via threats, coercion, and intimidation likely remained effective.

"Hm." Mateo glanced up at the high vaulted ceiling, dust particles dancing prominently in the cascading rays of light cutting through the dingy darkness. Then down at the floor.

Next to one of the beds, he noticed several splattered drops of blood, and moved closer to examine.

At length, he said, "Javier?"

The 'cleaner' promptly stepped forward, focusing in on what held Mateo's interest.

Mateo pointed at the traces of long-congealed blood. "You missed a spot."

"Never," he said. "As Diego mentioned, these accommodations have long been abandoned. Un-used. That could be from anything—the blood of a rat maybe."

"Or a child," said Mateo, drawing uncomfortable tension from all present. "No, I think Guadalupe or Hugo, or both used this space, and I think they used it recently . . ."

Mateo led his chair over to Diego, close enough to invade his personal space, and looked him in the eye. ". . . And I don't hesitate to tell you this— it *disgusts* me."

Diego blinked and looked away, clearing his throat. "I was only Guadalupe's lawyer."

"Of course you were . . . And I bet you still know all their names."

"Wh-Who's names?"

Mateo bit his lip and made for the door.

Javier ran to Mateo's side. "On to the plantation?"

"I don't care."

Retracing the path back to the beekeeper's apiary, Mateo called her to him. "If it's no trouble, I'd love a bottle of Genna's famous honey."

"Sí. Of course. As far as I'm concerned, everything here is yours."

Mateo leaned forward, and with some pain and effort, he stepped out of the hoverchair, meaning to walk back to his housing on his own two feet. "It seems you've made honey your livelihood, the bees, your family. So, from where I'm standing, this operation you've created is very much your own. But thank you for allowing me a visit."

"You are nothing like Guadalupe," whispered the woman.

"Something people keep telling me."

She glanced back at Diego and Javier, then lowered her voice even below a whisper. "Watch your back."

* * *

As Mateo limped back to his 'royal suite' to rest, Ana, Maria, and Lucia, taking turns helping him along, Diego and Javier peeled off and made for Bruno, still afar off in the training field with his fighters.

Mateo and the overseers exchanged guarded looks before they disappeared behind a corner of the palatial structure.

Maria set the injured Mateo on the side of the bed where the girls had slept the night previous.

"I know the doctor cleaned your wounds," Maria said. "But would you like another warm bath?"

Mateo smiled. "Only if you promise not to seduce me."

She returned the smile and glanced at her friends. "We will be good."

Mateo nodded. "Okay then."

As the girls attended him, this time as nurses rather than escorts, an innocent closeness bonded them as they talked.

Mateo learned that Ana was born on the other side of the continent, and her family immigrated here, before they were killed, and she was abducted as a young girl during a neighbor raid and passed through several sets of hands.

Lucia had run away from home as a child and worked in a gentlemen's club before getting an offer from the wrong people.

Maria had grown up here in the compound, but her parents had long since passed.

After hearing their stories, Mateo contemplated a while, their delicate strokes with wet washcloths soothing him nearly to sleep.

"What will you do when you leave here?" Mateo asked.

"Leave?" Lucia said. "Where would we go?"

"That's what I'm asking you," said Mateo. "You are free. Even now. No one is keeping you here. Guadalupe is dead."

"But Bruno," Ana said. "Diego. Javier . . . *And Hugo is still out there.*"

"Javier?" Mateo said. "Surely Javier is not keeping you here."

"This place is watched by many," Maria said. "Most of which you have not even met."

"Who?" Mateo asked.

"Guadalupe's people. Who do you think bought Lucia? Who abducted Ana . . . My parents? He has *many* people."

"He's dead," Mateo said again.

"Is he?" asked Maria, tears welling in her eyes.

"I will take you far from here," Mateo said. "If that's what you wish. So far, they won't find you . . . *All* of you. I will take you wherever you want.

You can find a trade, a life. A husband. Have children, raise families of your own."

"That won't be possible," Maria said distantly.

"What do you mean?" Mateo put a gentle finger on her chin, and her gaze eventually settled on his eyes.

Tears escaped down her cheek. "They have seen to it that none of us will ever bear new life in this world."

Mateo's heart sank, and he looked away.

"I always wished for a child," she said, "but in this country, even the love is depressing."

* * *

"Mateo . . . *Mateo, wake up.*" Her forceful voice reached inside with unruffled urgency, and his eyes snapped open.

"What is it, Ana?"

"Come." She stood next to Maria and Lucia as she beckoned. All three women were dressed and seemed ready to leave the grand hacienda.

Mateo, picking up on the resolve in their collective demeanor, quickly donned his cloak and followed them out the door into the still night. "What is the matter? Where are you taking me?"

"To the others," said Maria.

"The other—?"

"Servants. We feel there is something you must see."

"What? Is everything all right?"

Lucia gently urged him on from behind. "Nothing is ever all right here . . . nor has it ever been."

"Is it safe to wander the grounds in the middle of la noche?" he asked, almost rhetorically.

"Of course not," Lucia said. "Best be quiet."

Mateo appreciated her candor, and tried to keep his footfalls light.

Because of the darkness, Mateo's movements through the compound took on more urgency; the women set the pace.

Night insects chirped or rubbed their legs together to an echoing chorus under a vast canopy of captive stars from distant galaxies. Off to the left of the footpath, weathered headstones of varying age jutted from under brambles and unkempt grounds within the winding forested areas, like secrets dying to come to light.

The coterie passed under pines silvered with dew, a wash of crimson across the grass from dimmed window light escaping from the fighters' barracks.

"Where are we going?" Mateo whispered, though he could already guess, considering the general direction they headed.

"To the cliffs," said Ana. "Toward the sea."

"But this is not the way we went before."

"No. It isn't."

"Only the servants know of these paths," said Maria. "It's how we look out for one another when—" Her voice trailed off as though she suddenly thought better of finishing the thought.

Passing behind thick shrubbery and squeezing one-by-one through a tight gap in wood fencing, they progressed down a hardened dirt path, winding ever downward with hanging branches and jutting root systems causing them to duck, weave, or climb over. They all moved quickly, and the trek almost became a dance, the girls' nightgowns flowing in the starlight traces through the trees and past the boulders.

Several small lights appeared at a distance, and Mateo recognized the structures below them, though he had never seen them from above and behind. "The night servants' individual lodgings," he muttered. The simple, humble, stacked lodgings he had seen from the beach during the lineup.

"Shhh." Lucia put a finger to her lips and led the way, crouching, and sliding gracefully over the edge of a high retaining wall. Mateo gulped as he stepped back onto crumpling leaves and watched the other two follow and disappear out of sight. He tried to emulate their movements as he grasped the edge to lower himself down and jump to the stone sidewalk below but did so with considerably less grace . . . and silence.

"Shhh," Lucia repeated.

Mateo would have smiled, except for the next sounds that reached his ears; the stifled sobs and whimpering of children . . . *several* children.

The women led him closer toward the sounds; they knew exactly where to go; this wasn't the first time they had done this. No. Not even close.

When they arrived at the base of the target unit, Ana, Maria, and Lucia gestured for Mateo to look for himself. Mateo knew they didn't have to; their eyes were already wet, their hands trembling as though their bodies remembered past offenses and reacted compulsively.

Mateo took a moment to focus only on the dreadful cries and whimpers. But there was another sound too. The sound of a monster indulging his appetite.

Ever so slowly, Mateo tensed the muscles in his legs to raise his vantage point to the bottommost edge of the small round window, his hands gently caressing the rough and stringy wooden finish of the crude log housing as he went.

The dim interior lighting reached his eye, which widened at the disquieting scene. He stifled an audible response.

Four.

Two of the young children he had seen lined up on the beach that first evening crumpled over on the dingy floor. One child standing, facing the bed, and another obscured by the darkest of shadows—a heavy brute—seated on the edge with his hairy naked back toward the window.

Bruno Salazar. 'The Wall'.

Tears rose and gushed, and Mateo couldn't bear to witness for more than a few drawn out seconds. He turned and slid back down the coarse wall, a dogged vengeance building from deep within.

Ana hugged him warmly, yet he could feel her trembling, too. He knew she understood that vengeance that filled him to the brim, and he couldn't miss the fact that Maria and Lucia were clearly troubled, as well, but not only for the child abuse. They worried over what his reaction to it might be.

The young women could see it in his eyes, and they shook their heads, their lips sealed tight.

"DON'T," Ana mouthed, terror covering her face as she leaned away and took a step back.

Mateo stood defiantly to full stature, wishing it was more.

The women scattered like doves from a basket.

"BRUNO!" he shouted, turning to face the man inside the hovel. *"Get away from them!"*

Startled, the beast of a man spun about from off the bed, and instinctively ran for Mateo, reaching through the window and clawing at his neck and shoulders, yanking him through, lamps crashing, furniture groaning, flesh scraping, and children screaming.

* * *

"After careful deliberation with my colleagues and the majority of our shareholders, we have decided you are not a good fit to step in as Guadalupe's replacement."

"Diego?" Thrashed and battered with a scarred face, Mateo could barely open his eyes to discover he was prostrate in the grass in the middle of the open square, squinting at the lawyer. "You've . . . *decided?*"

"Sí."

Mateo glanced up past his silhouette into the morning sky. Never had he been lambasted or messed up with such brute force—not even by Hugo. Mateo's face throbbed, his many bruises and lacerations aching, and his limbs smarted with pain at each tiny movement of his body. "But . . . *The papers.*"

"What papers, mi amigo?" Diego opened his pad to show it empty.

"Disposing of legal documents. Now, that is a capital offense. And here I thought you had already submitted them to the board." With excruciating agony and effort, Mateo strained to sit upright, dabbing tenderly at his swollen eyes, forehead and cheeks, blood covering his fingers. Whether his or Bruno's, he couldn't be sure.

"Well, my friend," Diego said, "You are detached from reality, are you not? And as far as any legal documentation, I have absolutely no idea what you are talking about. Guadalupe's inheritance *would* have gone to his next of . . . *living* . . . kin, but unfortunately, he had none that we could locate with reasonable effort."

"So you are going to kill me then? Why didn't you do it already? Bruno got pretty damn close. Or were you hoping to do the honors yourself?" Just then, Mateo noticed Bruno standing nearby, seething like a bull before the matador's muleta. At least he had put on some clothes.

"Mateo, Mateo . . . I am only a lawyer." Diego turned and nodded to his compadres. Hugo stepped out from behind Bruno, bloodlust in his eyes as well. Any jolliness Mateo had perceived from their very first meeting had been buried in a wretched, guilty hatred, and the fear it imposed, indescribable.

"Great. Everyone's here." Two mad bulls, and Mateo in no shape to play bull fighter. Even if he were at optimal health, his physicality proved no match for either one of them. Mateo struggled to his feet, stepped back, and peered over at the women and children gathered. He didn't want them to see what might come next. The overseers would make an example of Mateo, and they would force the innocents to watch. Mateo mused that even Guadalupe would be tuning in from the not-so-great beyond to witness the spectacle, relations be damned. Even the cocineros and Bruno's fighting men had been invited to this unexpected party.

"You cannot kill someone who is already dead," Diego said, as Hugo approached Mateo. "And let's face it, you were finished the moment you stepped out of that limosina. All because of . . . *who you are*—you bring with you only entropy."

Hugo yanked Mateo's head back by the hair and punched him in the gut, folding him over. *I guess they both needed a turn.*

Diego laughed. "This was never for you to evaluate Guadalupe's properties, holdings, and other—shall we say—*assets*. No, Mateo, this was all set up as a way for Guadalupe's people to see if you would be a worthy candidate to take over such an empire, even Guadalupe's lifelong legacy. And in case you haven't caught the gist of where this is going . . . *You failed.*"

"Legacy?" Mateo uttered. "What legacy?"

"You . . . failed," Diego repeated. "But what were we thinking? Of course you could not adapt to our world."

Mateo nodded, blood rushing to his face, and out his nostrils. "I see."

Even more than defending himself from Hugo, Mateo wanted to wipe that smug look off Diego's face. "I only have one question before Hugo puts me in this well-manicured ground . . . in front of all these innocent children."

Diego leaned forward. "And what is that?"

Despite the searing pain in his belly, Mateo slowly stood upright until he reached his full height, glaring into Hugo's eyes through his scars and bruises. "What do you plan to do about . . . *them?*"

The overseers and Bruno's fighting men looked over at the night servants and groundskeepers standing nearby—Ana, Maria, and Lucia among them—and they all burst out in hearty laughter.

"What, Mateo?" Bruno sniggered, his eyes watering with amusement. "Are you expecting the women and children to protect you? The gardeners? Janitors?"

"No," Mateo said, slowly shaking his head. "Not them." He pointed to the horizon toward the ocean cliffs as a small fleet of freighters, shuttles, and space transport vessels lifted into view, and moved toward the gathering, flying low and surrounding everyone.

"Them."

Their respective boosters shot a violent wind over everyone, and the mixing noises from all the engines grew to a mind-numbing blare."

"Qué diablura es esta?" Diego muttered, eyeing the cockpits and pilot seats of each individual aircraft. There must have been over a dozen.

They must have emptied out the warehouse completely, Mateo thought. *Gracias a dios, and good for them.*

Even under the uproar, Mateo heard a growing buzzing noise. From a great distance in the other direction, a dark, shifting cloud appeared from over the tree line, emerging and morphing in shape until it came close enough to reveal itself as a swarm.

"Genna." Mateo grinned painfully, though curious how a swarm of bees with no stingers could possibly aid them.

However, as the insects approached, they started attacking only the overseers and Bruno's fighters, mostly leaving everyone else alone. And from the men's screams and overt reactions, it was clear the bees did, in fact, have stingers.

I guess she still had a batch or two of unmodified specimens, Mateo thought.

Notwithstanding the bees, the ruckus, and the shadows of the small fleet hovering just above their heads, Hugo still towered over Mateo and meant to finish what he started, grabbing him by the throat, and lifting him off the ground. "You wretch," he snarled, ignoring multiple stings.

Mateo took hold of his massive wrists, kicking and struggling to no avail. Things went blurry, and the relentless grip pushed in on his neck from all sides.

"Hugo!" shouted Maria. "You dash hand!"

Something thrashed Mateo and Hugo forcefully to one side, and it wasn't until they hit the ground that he realized Maria had struck Hugo in the side of the head with a shovel.

Hugo moved to fight back but was struck again from behind. Apparently, Lucia, too, had acquired a makeshift weapon from the groundskeepers.

Hugo's guards ran to his side with their machetes, but rather than protect him, they backed up Maria and Lucia, turning their blades on the man.

Both women pounded on Hugo's back until he lay unconscious, face smashed into the grass.

Mateo could easily see their fierce aggression was not merely to rescue him from Hugo so much as retribution for all the years of abuses endured.

Breathing hard, Mateo just sat there and watched, then nodded when they finally finished their work. "Where's Ana?" he asked, to which Maria and Lucia just searched the fighting and scattering crowd.

Swatting incessantly at the aggressive bees, Diego made for Mateo. The girls, bravely wielding their shovel and pick mattock, stood by him protectively.

"All of this madness will accomplish nothing!" Diego shouted. "It's over for you! Did you actually think you could run Guadalupe's trade empire? What would you know about it?" Diego spit at Mateo's feet. "Before I brought you here, you were nothing but a warehouse worker."

It was true Mateo had worked in a factory warehouse, but not merely as an assembly line peon, janitor, or machinist. For years, Mateo had been the floor manager of the multinational corporation, overseeing and assisting the work of more than 1,500 men and women, and in that time, he had learned a few things about managing people.

"Where's your girl?" Diego hissed.

"Ana." Mateo caught sight of her in Bruno's arms, and they were surrounded by his trained combatants.

Mateo made a gamble; he stood and grabbed a machete from one of Hugo's former guards, took Diego by the back of the head, and forced the blade's sharp cutting edge against the lawyer's neck. "Release her," Mateo growled.

Diego callously eyed him from the corner of his eye. *"There's* the Guadalupe in you."

"NOW!" Mateo pressed, grimacing at Bruno.

Diego bit into his bottom lip. "Even if he lets her go . . . you're surrounded."

Mateo wanted to have his friends execute a strafing run over the entire compound and eradicate the evil altogether, but unlike Guadalupe, he would show a little mercy.

He nodded at the guards, who took over, and secured Diego, Hugo, and Bruno, just as Genna emerged from behind them.

Bruno pushed Ana forward, knowing he'd be hacked to pieces if he didn't, and she collapsed in front of the brute.

Mateo could barely walk, but he helped her as best he could a safe distance away from the dangerous ones before they collapsed together. She hugged Mateo ever so gently as they repositioned themselves carefully, sitting upright on the lawn.

Together, with Ana, Maria, Lucia, and everyone else, they just watched the bedlam unfold. Javier was nowhere to be seen.

"Are these not your genetically modified bees?" Mateo asked Genna, attempting to manage the pain from simply sitting there.

"To modify a specimen," she said, "One must first start with a pure creator batch. I simply couldn't bring myself to waste the original lines. In fact, I've been experimenting with them for years. They have 170 olfactory or 'smell' receptors, but only 10 gustatory ones, you know, for 'taste'. They use their extraordinary senses to detect chemical signals, including pheromones from their surroundings, and, wouldn't you know it, the overseers put off a different aroma than everyone else around here. All that expensive cologne—my bees like it too. *Or hate it.* I'm not quite sure which."

Mateo thought a moment, "Well, that whole different hive of killer bees made all the difference."

"No. They're not killers," Genna corrected him. *"Defenders."*

"I see," Mateo said. "Why don't they attack me?"

Genna smiled. "Well, you're quite a new smell, aren't you? I haven't introduced your scent to them."

"Remind me to stay on your good side."

Everyone smiled.

"How did you know to come?" Mateo asked.

"The girls. They told me right after Bruno took you . . . Truthfully, I feared I would be too late. I couldn't see another casualty at the hands of these monstruos. And honestly, I wasn't sure this would work." She giggled. "Día feliz."

After the bees had done their work, Genna dulcified them and led them back to their hives with a specially concocted lemongrass swarm lure she had been hiding under sealed lid in her ragged cloak.

Diego watched Mateo from behind the guards' machetes a way off and would wait there until the authorities arrived.

When Mateo could handle it, he, with the help of Guadalupe's former harem, stood upright to hobble to a recovery bed. As he passed the lawyer, he said, "Tell me, Diego, what is it that transforms a man into such a monster as Guadalupe?"

"Why?" Diego scoffed. "What has he done but build a lucrative trade empire?"

"I don't know, given heed to seducing spirits? Doctrines of devils?"

"None of this will matter," said Diego. "Money is more powerful than morals."

"I've called on a few of my friends from the factory," Mateo said, staring him down. "*My* factory. I'm in the process of buying it, you see—I can afford it now. I made that call shortly after you gave me the number and tracked down some lawyers of my own—before you destroyed all that legal documentation, that is. They, too, have been tracking me with their drones, and everything transpiring here. If you look into the sky, perhaps you might even be able to spot some of them."

Diego gritted his teeth in anger.

Mateo continued, "The warehouse I worked in is one of the few businesses around here that Guadalupe didn't already own. I feel like it was a wise investment, don't you? I mean, I managed the floor all those years, and, after all, those are people I can trust."

"Your call to the accountant." Diego finally realized. "The missing 94 million credits . . . you—"

"Transferred them to Felipe," Mateo said. "*My* . . . lawyer."

"But how did you acquire—?"

"I have friends too, Diego. *Talented* friends."

"Felipe? What—?"

"Yes. I transferred the credits with very specific instructions," Mateo added. "And how did *you* know about the transfer? You're not listed on those accounts—or you're not supposed to be . . . Whatever. We can have the authorities look into it. Anyway, thanks for getting me the number."

"You insolent piece of—"

"Adios, Diego." Mateo turned to the girls.

And finally—lacking the suppressive influence of the overseers—the girls managed to smile at Diego, Bruno, and Hugo, as they assisted Mateo past them.

"I have a question," Mateo said to the girls. "The same question I asked you all before: What will you do when you leave this place?"

Each of the girls peered up at the freighters, shuttles, and space transport vessels from Mateo's factory, putting some real thought into the question.

"Leave?" Lucia said, as she did before. "But where would we go?"

* * *

Only now did Mateo notice that the far reaches of Guadalupe's compound bordered on the pastoral lands and outer edges of the trade streets he had visited so many times before, unwitting. He mused at the thought of Guadalupe's dark-haired women, broken-willed children, and the progress they had all made in finding some scrap of real meaning in the world, despite their ordeals. Scraps that, Mateo hoped, would eventually become feasts.

Peering into the shallow valley ahead with its market bazaar and vendors hawking their freshly grown, caught, or crafted goods, and the vast sea beyond, Mateo wondered how long it had truly been since his ancestors broke atmosphere and claimed this land for their own. He also wondered if he would venture a ride out of that same atmosphere to explore other places (as Ana kept coaxing him to try).

He rubbed his face and neck, still healing from his skirmishes with Hugo and Bruno at the hacienda weeks previous, both of whom awaited trial from some jail cell across the village, along with Diego and many of the others.

With a scar like Bruno's, only this one earned and worn with valor,

Mateo strolled down the side of a long dirt road. Although almost fully recovered, he still walked with a limp in his left leg, which seemed to worsen on the downhill stride.

Entering the market square to purchase some fresh fruit and vegetables for one of Ana's new soup recipes, he was approached and stopped by a friendly merchant, who stared as if comparing Mateo's likeness against an old memory.

"Excuse me," said the man, "but did you know *Guadalupe,* the renowned businessman? The tradesman?"

"I knew *of* him," said Mateo. "Like everyone on this side of the continent, of course I've heard the name."

"It's just that there has been much talk here in the bazaar—recent stories from the compound, some of them originating from . . . the former staff. And you look hauntingly familiar. In fact, the resemblance is uncanny. You . . . you were his nephew, no?"

I'm out of that family, Mateo thought. *Ashamed to even share his blood.*

"His nephew?" Mateo shook his head. *"No.* No, I carry no relation to the famosa Guadalupe."

The End

About the Author

Brian C Hailes has written/illustrated over 60 titles, including four illustrated novels, Hotel California, Avila, Defender of Llyans, and Blink, two graphic novels, Devil's Triangle, and Dragon's Gait, and many short stories and children's books. He also illustrated several Girl of the Year books for American Girl, and Continuum (Arcana Comics). In 2002, he won the L. Ron Hubbard Illustrators of the Future award and is now an official judge for the contest. His artwork has been featured in the 2017-2024 editions of Infected By Art. He currently lives in Salt Lake City with his wife and four boys, where he continues to write, draw, paint, and produce videos regularly. His work can be seen at:

HailesArt.com
DrawItWithMe.com
Instagram: drawitwithmeofficial
Facebook: drawitwithme
ArtStation: bchailes

DEVIL'S TRIANGLE
THE COMPLETE GRAPHIC NOVEL
HAILES   CASSELMAN

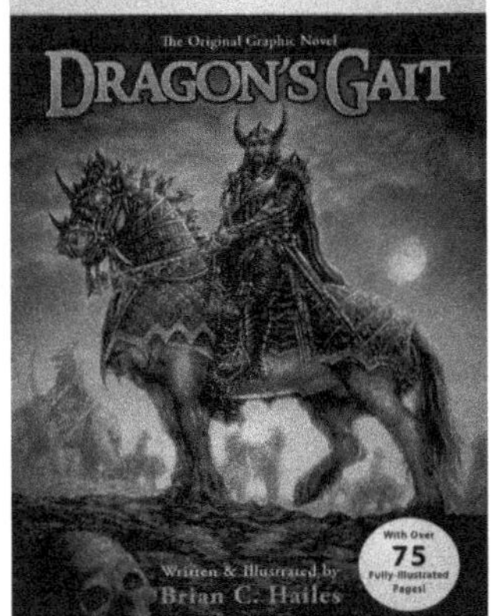

The Original Graphic Novel
DRAGON'S GAIT
With Over 75 Fully-Illustrated Pages!
Written & Illustrated by
Brian C. Hailes

An Illustrated Science Fiction Novel
AVILA
HAILES   DEFENDI
COMING SOON!

DRAW IT WITH ME: THE
DYNAMIC
FEMALE FIGURE
BRIAN C HAILES

DRAW IT WITH ME A
STUDY OF THE
HUMAN FORM
BRIAN C HAILES

KAMIKAZI
BRIAN C HAILES   JOHN ENGLISH

DRAW IT WITH ME: THE
ELEGANT
FEMALE FORM
An Intimate Study of the Beautiful Feminine
Figure in Varied Chic & Classical Poses
BRIAN C HAILES

COLOR MY OWN
HALLOWEEN
STORY
AN IMMERSIVE, CUSTOMIZABLE
COLORING BOOK
FOR KIDS
(THAT RHYMES)
by BRIAN C HAILES

DON'T GO NEAR THE
CROCODILE
PONDS
BRIAN C HAILES

IF I WERE A
SPACEMAN
A RHYMING ADVENTURE THROUGH THE COSMOS
BRIAN C HAILES
ILLUSTRATIONS BY TEYH LUADTHONG

HERE, THERE BE
MONSTERS
A RHYMING QUEST TO FIND TERRORS OF LEGEND & MYTH
BRIAN C HAILES
ILLUSTRATIONS BY TEYH LUADTHONG

Can We Be Friends?
STORY BY EDIE NEW
ART BY CINDY HAILES

EPIC EDGE
PUBLISHING